B55 060 822 X

Scu(

ROTHERHAM LIBRARIES AND NEIGHBOURHOOD HUBS

15 AUG 2023

FRANKLIN WATTS
LONDON•SYDNEY

Maya and Rosa looked at all the eggs.

"Look," said Mum.

"The big eggs will hatch into ducklings.

They will grow into ducks.

The small eggs will hatch into chicks.

They will grow into hens."

"Can we help look after them?"
asked Maya and Rosa.
Mum nodded.
"We need to keep them warm."

A week went by.

Mum held the big eggs

up to the light, one by one.

"Good," she said.

Then she looked at the small eggs, one by one.

"Oh dear," she said.

"Just one egg will hatch.

I will put it with the big eggs."

Two weeks went by.

The big eggs began to hatch.

Out came three yellow ducklings.

"What shall we call them?"
asked Maya.

"Barry, Garry and Larry,"
said Rosa.

The next day, the small egg
began to hatch.
Out came a chick. It was yellow,
just like the ducklings.

"We can call her Hetty,"
said Maya.

Hetty grew into a hen and the ducklings grew into ducks. Every day, they went to play down by the pond.

The ducks had big flat feet
to pad about.
Hetty tried to pad, too,
but she did not have flat feet.

The ducks went for a swim
in the pond.
Hetty went, too.
She tried to swim but
she did not have strong legs.

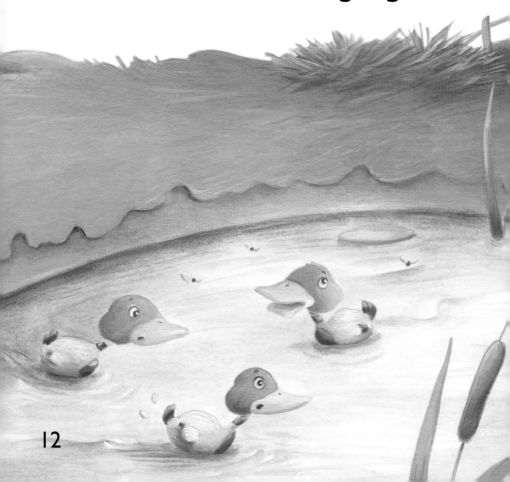

"I am going to put Hetty

in the hen-house," said Mum.

"Hetty is a hen, not a duck."

But Hetty didn't want to go.

That night, the ducks quacked and Hetty squawked.
They kept everyone awake.

In the morning, Mum opened
the hen-house door.
Hetty ran out to see the ducks.
"Hetty is a hen but she thinks
she's a duck," said Maya.

Mum smiled.

"Hetty wants to live with
the ducks," she said.

"She is a hen-duck."

So Hetty went to live with
the ducks.
Mum made her
somewhere to sleep.
The ducks were happy.
And Hetty was happy, too.

Story trail

Start

Start at the beginning of the story trail. Ask your child to retell the story in their own words, pointing to each picture in turn to recall the sequence of events.

Independent Reading

This series is designed to provide an opportunity for your child to read on their own. These notes are written for you to help your child choose a book and to read it independently.

In school, your child's teacher will often be using reading books which have been banded to support the process of learning to read. Use the book band colour your child is reading in school to help you make a good choice. *The Hen-Duck* is a good choice for children reading at Green Band in their classroom to read independently.

The aim of independent reading is to read this book with ease, so that your child enjoys the story and relates it to their own experiences.

About the book

Hetty the Hen-Duck hatches with the ducklings – and she refuses to believe she is not one of them!

Before reading

Help your child to learn how to make good choices by asking:
"Why did you choose this book? Why do you think you will enjoy it?"
Look at the cover together and ask: "What do you think the story will be about?" Support your child to think of what they already know about the story context. Read the title aloud and ask: "What do you think a hen-duck might be?"

Remind your child that they can try to sound out the letters to make a word if they get stuck.

Decide together whether your child will read the story independently or read it aloud to you.

During reading

If reading aloud, support your child if they hesitate or ask for help by telling the word. Remind your child of what they know and what they can do independently.

If reading to themselves, remind your child that they can come and ask for your help if stuck.

After reading

Support comprehension by asking your child to tell you about the story. Use the story trail to encourage your child to retell the story in the right sequence, in their own words.

Help your child think about the messages in the book that go beyond the story and ask: "Do you think Hetty is happier when she is with the ducks rather than the hens? Why/why not?"

Give your child a chance to respond to the story: "Did you have a favourite part? Why do you think Hetty felt more like a duck than a hen? Can you think of any other stories where one animal feels like a different animal?"

Extending learning

Help your child understand the story structure by using the same story context and adding different elements. "Let's make up a new story about an animal who feels like a different animal. What kind of animal will you choose? What other animal does your animal feel like?" In the classroom, your child's teacher may be teaching polysyllabic words (words with more than one syllable). There are many in this book that you could look at with your child, for example: in/to, duck/lings, ye/llow, to/ge/ther, eve/ry/one, a/wake, morn/ing, some/where, hen-/house, ha/ppy.

Franklin Watts
First published in Great Britain in 2020
by The Watts Publishing Group

Copyright © The Watts Publishing Group 2020

Series Editors: Jackie Hamley and Melanie Palmer
Series Advisors: Dr Sue Bodman and Glen Franklin
Series Designer: Peter Scoulding

A CIP catalogue record for this book is
available from the British Library.

ISBN 978 1 4451 7067 1 (hbk)
ISBN 978 1 4451 7069 5 (pbk)
ISBN 978 1 4451 7068 8 (library ebook)

Printed in China

Franklin Watts
An imprint of
Hachette Children's Group
Part of The Watts Publishing Group
Carmelite House
50 Victoria Embankment
London EC4Y 0DZ

An Hachette UK Company
www.hachette.co.uk

www.franklinwatts.co.uk